JONATHAN'S FRIENDS

JONATHAN'S FRIENDS

W. B. PARK

G. P. Putnam's Sons · New York

Copyright © 1977 by W.B. Park
All rights reserved. Published simultaneously
in Canada by Longman Canada, Toronto.
Printed in the United States of America

LIBRARY OF CONGRESS
CATALOGING IN PUBLICATION DATA

Park, W.B. Jonathan's friends.
Summary: A young boy is reluctant to accept his older brother's
explanation about the tooth fairy, Santa Claus, and elves.
[1. Brothers and sisters—Fiction] I. Title.
PZ7.P22145Jo [E]   77-5041
ISBN 0-399-20604-3

To my mother, who taught me how to believe,
and my dad, the most decent man I've ever known

As always, Michael was swinging
and Jonathan was pushing.
"Jonathan," said Michael, "it's time you found out."
Michael was feeling very grown-up.
"Found out what?" Jonathan asked.
"The truth about make-believe," said Michael.

"You mean about fairies and elves?" Jonathan asked.
"Uh-huh," said Michael, "Things like that aren't really real."
 Jonathan's eyes grew larger.

"But, Michael, who leaves me a silver dollar
    when I lose a tooth?" Jonathan asked.
"Mom and Dad," Michael told him. "Where would
    fairies get money?"

"From the elves," Jonathan said.

"Elves aren't real either," said Michael.

"They are too," Jonathan said. "I hear them dancing in our attic at night." Michael laughed.

"Jonathan, those are just mice running around."

"Do you still believe in witches and ghosts
   on Halloween?" Michael asked.
"I sure do," Jonathan said. "Don't you?"
"Of course not," said Michael. "Those are just people
   dressed up in costumes."

"Michael, you're just being mean!" Jonathan said.
"No, I'm not," Michael said. "It's time you learned
  what's real."

"Well, I know the Easter Bunny is real," Jonathan said.
"He hides Easter eggs and jelly beans all over the
house at Easter time."
"Mom and Dad do that the night before," said Michael.

"Stop talking like that!" Jonathan said.
"Okay," said Michael and they didn't say anything
the rest of the way home.

After supper Michael was busy as usual,
  showing Jonathan how to do things his way.
"Michael," Jonathan said.
"What," Michael answered.
"I still believe in all those things."

Michael didn't say anything.
On the way up to bed Jonathan asked, "Michael,
don't you believe in anything?"
"Nope," said Michael.

"Not even Santa Claus?" Jonathan asked.

"Nope," said Michael, "not even Santa Claus."

"Gosh," Jonathan said.

"You see, Jonathan, parents and adults and people
   like that make up those things," Michael explained.
"But why?" Jonathan asked.
"When you're as old as I am, you'll understand."
   Michael turned out the light. "Then you'll think
   just like I do."

"Oh, no I won't, Michael," Jonathan said.
  But Michael didn't hear him.
  He was already asleep.